Summer
of the
Lost Limb

". . . I will lead them in paths that they have not known . . .
these things will I do . . . and not forsake them" (Isaiah 42:16).

Summer
of the
Lost Limb

by Janis Good

illustrated by Elizabeth Cates

Published by Christian Recollections
Peace Valley Road, Route 1, Box 351
Mount Solon, Virginia 22843

Printed by Banta, Harrisonburg, Virginia

ISBN 0-9640365-5-X

Dedicated
to
Mary Rohrer
and
Maggie Koogler

Acknowledgments

Special thanks to the nieces
of Mary Rohrer and Maggie Koogler:
Esther Wenger
Mattie Wenger
Naomi Showalter
Blanche Showalter
Betty Horst

Without their assistance, this story could not have been brought to the printed page.

Photography by
My Hometown

Contents

Preface

Mary, at the age of 89, had a story to tell which I was eager to hear. The account of a country operation performed in 1908 on Mary's familiar kitchen table has intrigued me from the very first time I heard about it. At first I intended to write only a short story, but the story grew and grew until it became a book.

While nieces and grandnieces quilted around the quilt frame in Mary's home, they helped to piece the scraps of this story together. There were still actual remnants in Mary's home left from that happening 85 years ago which caused the story to leap into life. Nestled in a corner of Mary's bedroom were a child-size wheelchair, tiny crutches, the initial wooden limb, and a ragged, but valuable Steiff bear.

Mary searched in her chest of drawers for documents of doctor bills and magazine clippings about Steiff bears, Theodore Roosevelt and his hunting expedition, the artificial limb inventor, and favorite songs her father sang, etc. Her collection of such were a tremendous aid in piecing the story together.

Mary's spunk shone through in spite of a failing memory and physical setbacks as she shared this story. Her sister Maggie, at 102 years, had an amazing memory of incidents. Mary's brother, John, also helped to furnish some information before he passed away.

The people, events, and places in this story are true. However, the placement of some incidents have been arranged for plot movement. Where accounts given me did not agree, I have endeavored to take the most logical direction.

The 1908 period was researched to recapture the times as they were then. Also, I have endeavored to portray the life and culture of the Old Order Mennonite faith as it was practiced then and now.

The times of sitting around quilts or a table with the Rohrer family where we became acquainted will always be cherished memories. I have been deeply impressed by the loving care shown to Mary and Maggie in their sunset years by those who are truly their loved ones.

My desire is that Mary's courage, persistence, and faith in God will encourage others to keep going despite difficulty and trials they experience.

Janis Good

Mary's Family

The Rohrer household in 1908 contained many members. To avoid confusion in mentioning each person and their ages in the story, they are listed here with their age in 1908.

Israel Hess Rohrer (Papa)	48 years
Lydia Ann Rhodes Rohrer (Mama)	46 years
Ava Myra (sister)	21 years
Henry Warren (married brother)	20 years
Maggie Edith (sister)	18 years
Amos Daniel (brother)	16 years
William Rhodes (brother)	14 years
Anna May (Annie, sister)	12 years
Ella Amelia (sister)	10 years
John Sanford (brother)	8 years
Mary Esther (main character)	5 years
Frank Israel (brother)	3 years
Mabel Rebecca (baby sister)	5 months
Anna Hess Rohrer (grandmother)	82 years
Mattie L. Rohrer (aunt)	40 years

Mary's lively feet kept her airborne most of the time.

1
Lively Feet

The sun crept high into the sky, spreading hot, late-summer rays over the Shenandoah Valley of Virginia. A cloudless August sky offered little hope for rain to fill Dry River's rocky streambed. All winter and spring, water had flowed down the Allegheny Mountain streams into the river basin. This summer of 1908, as in any other summer, Dry River would prove true to its name and cease to flow until winter. Then melting ice, sleet and snow would flush down the riverbed past villages and farms.

Near Dry River's banks, flat fields soaked up the sunrays for a good harvest. Within the square farmhouse, the Rohrer family scurried about with work necessary for the care and keeping of a farm and large family.

And a big family it was—Grandmother, Aunt Mattie, Papa and Mama Rohrer, and their ten children. One of the children, Henry, had married and moved to his own home with his new wife. That left nine children to fill the dwelling Papa Rohrer had built in 1900.

Slim five-year-old Mary, third to the youngest, sprinted across the yard in a tag game with brothers and sisters. Her pigtails bounced under her printed sunbonnet as she pressed forward trying to catch someone. This moment of play was one of the activities she and her family enjoyed between the many chores. Picnics, swimming, singing, and visiting were other activities they intertwined with work.

On Sunday morning, Mary and her family, plainly dressed in Sunday best, squeezed into two or more buggies. Pet, the horse from Mama's home, trotted off carrying Papa, Mama, Mary and the younger ones in the family to the little Mennonite church. Then home they would come to a delicious dinner and an afternoon of rest. A day of rest and worship paid off, for on Monday the busy days started again and continued right up through Saturday.

On this hot August afternoon, the sun-scorched grass crackled under Mary's bare feet as she chased her brother, John.

"Mary," Mama called from the back door. "Mar-r-ry."

"Yes," she answered, still chasing John. "Gotcha!" She gave him a sound tap, then spun around and sped to the house, keeping an eye across her shoulder.

"Mary," Mama called again. "Come now and help. It's most too hot to play tag."

Mary pounced before Mama, landing with both feet square in place. Her eyes danced with excitement. "It's fun, Mama!"

"Please go to the springhouse and bring back butter," said Mama. "Supper will be ready soon. Ella, come set the table."

Mary's lively feet kept her airborne most of the time as she skipped past Mama's flower garden. The whiff of a late summer rose caught her nose. She paused a moment smelling its sweet fragrance. This summer had been so good. Would it always be so?

Mary straightened and peered with hand over her brow toward the little school in the distance. She could not really see it, but she knew it was just beyond the tree-lined banks of the river. Not this fall, but next, she would be old enough to walk to school alongside her big brothers and sisters and the neighbor Shifflet children.

One more year! What a long time to wait. But someday she knew she would be with them. What fun it was going to be swinging her lunch pail as she crossed the swinging bridge and followed the road to the schoolhouse.

That butter for Mama! Mary picked up her heels and ran to the springhouse. She stepped inside and stooped to sip the water gurgling from the pipe. Grandfather Rohrer had hollowed the pipe from tree branches years ago when he first moved here from Pennsylvania. He had cemented the hollowed branches together to pipe water into the springhouse.

Mary searched among the milk jars in the water trough and found the butter container. She drew her dripping hands across her face and sighed, "Whew, that feels good."

Just then she heard Maggie in the loom room on the third level of the springhouse. She must see what her older sister was weaving today. Clasping the butter container, she stepped up into the second level where the washing was done. She scurried up the next flight of stairs, noticing the scent of smoked hams hanging on the walls in the two levels beyond this yet.

"So it's you, Mary," Maggie said without turning, her fingers skillfully weaving the strands into the rug.

"How'd you know it was me?"

"The sound of your feet," Maggie said chuckling.

"What a pretty rug that will be," said Mary, fingering the colored strips woven into the rug.

"Think so?"

Mary nodded.

"Mar-r-y-y," Mama called in the distance.

"You'd better scramble, girl," Maggie grinned. "That butter might melt out here anyhow in this heat."

"Mar-r-y-y," Mama called again. "Come for supper. Tell Maggie to come too."

"You run on, Mary," Maggie said, "I'll finish this row and be in shortly."

Mary whisked down the stairs and across the yard. She darted by Papa on his way to the springhouse with cans of milk for cooling. He was singing, "There's a City of Light, 'mid the stars we are told," like always when the chores were finished. She hurried up the steps and into the kitchen.

"Here's the butter, Mama," she said holding out the container.

Mary felt the warmth radiating from the tomato jars cooling on the counter as she washed at the sink.

She slipped into her place at the table and tried to amuse Baby Mabel fussing for her supper. Mama set heaping bowls of food on the table while Grandmother Rohrer filled 12 glasses circled around the long table. Gradually the family members appeared and found their places at the table.

"Yummy! Corn on the cob," Mary exclaimed. "No wonder we needed butter!"

"There's plenty of corn, tomatoes, potatoes and beef," Mama said smiling as she set dishes on the table.

The door banged. Maggie appeared in the doorway and gently slid into the last empty chair. All the Rohrers were present except Aunt Mattie who was working away and Henry who had married. Each head bowed for the customary silent prayer before meals.

Mary tried hard to keep her mind on praying but her thoughts kept wandering to the little schoolhouse. How could she pass the time for one slow year?

Papa's deep sigh indicated the end of prayer and the family passed the platter of corn and other dishes.

"That's the last of the butter, Israel," Mama said to Papa. "We need lots of butter when corn is in season."

Mary bit into the golden corn, tasting the sweetness on her tongue, but her thoughts were far away. She chewed the corn and daydreamed.

She saw herself running through the fields toward Dry River. She crossed the swinging bridge and frolicked down the river road toward the little school. She took another bite of corn and chewed slowly. In her mind she stood before Rushville School by the side of Dry River. When would the moment finally come when she would actually be there in real life rather than in daydreams?

2

The Accident

The butter churn clattered and clanked until a large lump of butter lay smothered in buttermilk at the bottom of the churn. Mary loved these evenings Papa churned butter with baby Mabel on his knee or another young child, perhaps even herself. He would bounce the child and sing in rhythm with his churning.

> *Baby bye*
> *Here's a fly*
> *Let us watch him you and I*
> > *How he crawls*
> > > *Up the walls*
> > > > *Yet he never falls!*

> *I believe with six such legs*
> *You and I could walk on eggs*
> > *There he goes*
> > > *On his toes*
> > > > *Tickling baby's nose!*

Baby Mabel giggled when Papa touched her nose and was often asleep until Papa had finished churning. Then Mama washed and salted the butter and placed it into molds. Once again the springhouse cooled much butter for the big family. It was hard to believe life could be any different than now.

In the later afternoon of August 12, 1908, Mary skipped along the driveway toward the barn where her brothers and sisters were doing chores. Skippity skip. She watched birds wing their way homeward above golden cornfields. Skippity skip. To the west the sun slipped behind a cloud hovering just above the Allegheny Mountains.

A song burst forth as she skipped. "La, de-de-da-a-a." In the distance Papa's singing in the barn where he was feeding and milking cows floated toward her. She glanced toward the barn, but not seeing Papa, she turned her attention to the horses and feed grinder just ahead, beside the granary.

Skippity skip. Skippity skip. She took one last hop, landing with both feet squarely in place. Round and round the horses plodded, turning the grinder wheel that ground the corn into feed.

She tugged her sunbonnet forward to keep the wind from blowing her hair over her face. Another hop brought her very close to her older brothers, Amos and William. She watched them lift sacks of dry ear corn and dump it into the opening at the top of the grinder. The grinder gobbled up the corn, like a great hungry animal. From the spout, finely ground feed spilled into waiting barrels.

Mary glanced off in the distance and watched her sister, Annie, nearing the lamb's pen. She tossed her pigtails over her shoulders and turned back to the interesting activity before her. Clip clop, clip clop.

The horses trudged on and on, circling to make the grinder work. Clip clop, clip clop. Round and round they went. What fun a ride would be she thought. She knew she could do it if she waited till the horses had just passed her. Then she would run and catch hold of the tongue that fastened to them. At just the right moment she dashed forward, caught the tongue, and climbed up while the contraption was still in motion. She seated herself on the tongue and kicked her legs back and forth, back and forth, in time to the clip clop of the horses' feet.

Round and round the horses plodded, turning the grinder wheel . . . (Courtesy of Betty Horst).

"La-la-de-de-da" she sang as she turned round and round with the horses. "La-de-de-da-a." She watched Amos and William work steadily pouring in ear corn and carrying the ground corn off to the granary nearby.

Suddenly Mary felt a horrible pinch on her foot, like a giant animal holding her foot in its mouth. She stopped singing and screamed. Her foot was caught in the corner leg of the grinder which anchored the grinder to the ground. Desperately she clung to the tongue hoping to save herself from further injury.

The horses slowed and the grinder wheel slowed until it stopped. Mary looked down at her leg as her brothers gently freed her from the machine. What had happened? She looked again, her eyes opening wide. Could it really be? The foot at the end of her right leg was missing! She heard the excited chatter of her loved ones gathering around her. There were Papa, Mama, Maggie, and the others, but she could not manage to concentrate on what they were saying.

"What happened?" Annie gasped, hurrying toward the cluster of family surrounding Mary.

"She's hurt, bad."

Mary felt herself cradled between Mama and Maggie as they whisked her to the house. She saw Mama blinking back tears and muttering, "Poor, poor Mary." She heard Papa directing orders in his very firm way when he meant business.

"We need Doctor Turner right away," he called over his shoulder to one of the boys. "Run fast to Tom Heatwoles and call the doctor."

Mama and Maggie eased Mary into the house and onto the couch. Mary lay white and still, staring at the ceiling. Her mind tried to focus but everything blurred into a gray cloud. Why was everyone gathering around her? Why the whispering and tears in their eyes?

Mary blinked her eyes, trying to bring the blur to focus. What had happened? There were horses grinding corn. She remembered herself climbing onto the crossbar and the gleeful ride. Then it had happened.

Tick tock, tick tock. She heard the clock ticking away the minutes. Over in the little town of Hinton, Doctor Turner would hear of this and be on the way to help her. Surely he could help in some way.

Closing her eyes, Mary breathed deeply. In her mind a picture of the little schoolhouse of Rushville floated towards her on a dreamy cloud. She forced her droopy eyelids open wide. How could she possibly walk to school with only one leg?

Tick tock, tick tock. The minutes ticked so slowly. The kitchen door banged and the brother who had gone to call the doctor at a neighbor's telephone appeared at the door.

"How is she?" he asked.

"She doesn't have pain," Mama said dabbing at the tears which kept gathering in the corners of her eyes.

"Did you get Doctor Turner?" asked Papa.

"Yes, he's on the way. I called Henry too and he's also coming."

Tick tock, tick tock. Would the doctor ever come? Far in the distance Mary heard the faint clip clop of a horse. Closer and closer it came. Clippity clop, clippity clop. While children peered from the windows watching the doctor's arrival, Mama wiped Mary's brow with a cool cloth. In a moment Doctor Turner stood at the doorway, hat in one hand and black bag in the other.

3

Kitchen Surgery

Doctor Turner placed his black bag by her side and knelt to examine her injured limb. Mary watched lines in his brow deepen like ridges in a freshly plowed field. The warmth of the doctor's hand on her shoulder calmed her. She drew a deep breath. Surely he could help right this horrible situation.

"Do you hurt?" The doctor's soft voice broke into her thoughts.

"No," she answered. "I just want my bed."

"Amazing," Papa whispered.

"She is in shock," Doctor Turner explained. "That is why she feels so little pain."

Mary rolled her head to the side, seeing the doctor's back, tall and straight, as he talked to Papa and Mama.

"The hospital is 200 miles away," he said, "which is too far for Mary who needs help now."

She lay quietly, dazed at all that had happened. Yesterday she had lively, active feet. Tonight she needed a hospital which was too far away. What was

Doctor Turner saying to Papa and Mama?

Doctor Turner spoke softly, "Mary needs surgery to remove more of her leg because the tendons and muscles have contracted far up her leg."

"Poor, poor Mary will never walk again!" Mama sobbed into her apron. "My poor, poor Mary!"

Doctor Turner turned to face Papa. "I'm needing two more doctors to assist me," he said. "Will someone please call Doctor Ralston at Mount Clinton and Doctor Payne in Dayton? Please tell them to come quickly."

There was a shuffle within the room. The kitchen door creaked on its hinges and banged shut. Mary's eyelids fluttered shut. She opened them dreamily and saw Mama dabbing at her eyes with a handkerchief as she rocked Baby Mabel. Again Mary's eyelids closed slowly. She forced her eyes open again. There stood her brothers and sisters clustered together, their wide-opened eyes darting to and fro. They jammed their hands into overall pockets or twisted

In the distance she heard the sound of horses' feet . . .

them in the folds of full skirts. And there was Henry. When had he arrived?

Mary looked past the doctor and saw Grandmother rocking in her chair with her worn German Bible on her lap. Her lips moved in her native language. Mary knew God could understand Grandmother's prayer even if she could not.

"What can I do to help?" Papa asked.

"We need a lot of light and a table," the Doctor said.

Mary's eyes would not stay open, but she heard the scraping of table legs on the floor as the table was positioned under the mantle where three lamps were arranged in a row. She heard the tinkling of the glass as Papa removed the lampshades and lit each one. Her eyes opened when she felt herself being carried to the table under the bright glow of lamps. She blinked as the light flickered on the walls around her.

"I want my bed," she muttered sleepily.

"The doctor will help you," Papa said, smoothing her brow.

Mary felt the cloth go around her thigh as the doctor slowly turned the tourniquet to stop the flow of blood.

"Could someone hold this tourniquet for me?" Doctor Turner asked.

"I will," Henry said, stepping forward and placing his big hand lovingly but firmly on the tightly twisted cloth that stopped the flow of blood in his little sister's leg.

Mary looked up into his eyes. Why did he, her only married brother, look at her so tenderly and soberly? Was Bertie, his wife, at home? Likely. Very soon

Henry and Bertie would have a new little one to join them. This new little one would call her Aunt Mary. How she was looking forward to being aunt for the first time.

She allowed her eyes to close on their own accord. If only this had never happened. If only she could awaken and find this a nightmare. But when she opened her eyes, it was true. There was the doctor, her family, Henry and the lamps. It was true.

In the distance she heard the sound of horses' feet on the road. Clippity clop, clippity clop. Clippity clippity clippity clop. Her family heard them also and stepped aside, making a path for the doctors.

The doctors arrived and arranged themselves around her. Mary felt little pain as they worked. Tick tock, tick tock. Time crept so slowly. One hour passed. Two hours. Still the doctors worked over her. As time passed she saw Amos, William, and John taking turns holding the lamp for the doctors.

Then Henry held the lamp high over the table. Mary blinked under the bright glow and closed her eyes again. Suddenly there was a clatter and a thud. Mary's eyes shot open. The lamp which had been shining in her eyes was gone and the doctors were bending over someone on the floor.

"What happened?" Henry sputtered.

"You fainted," Doctor Turner answered. "Are you all right?"

"I'm fine," Henry said, sitting up.

"Take it easy now," the doctor advised. "Someone else can hold the lamp."

"I'll hold it," the neighbor, Aldine Knicely, offered.

"Fine," said the doctor. "We still have work to do."

Sometimes she drifted into a brief sleep, only to awaken to the sound of the clock as the minutes ticked onward. Tick tock, tick tock. When would this nightmare end? Tick tock, tick tock. Finally the clock on the wall donged the hour. Dong, dong, dong nine times.

"Finished," Doctor Turner said, patting her arm and reaching for his handkerchief to wipe his damp forehead. "I'll be back to check on you tomorrow and every day to see how you are doing."

Mary blinked sleepily as she watched the three doctors disappear through the door. The family and neighbors who gathered around her blurred to her vision.

"I'm so sleepy," she muttered.

"Go to sleep, Mary," Mama said, patting her shoulder while she wiped a tear from her own eyes with the corner of her apron.

Mary felt Papa's strong arms lift her from the hard kitchen table and gently prop her on the sofa. The kitchen door creaked on its hinges. Even though she could not see them, she knew the neighbors were leaving.

Dreamclouds swooped down and carried her into dreamland. In her dream she saw the swinging bridge spanning Dry River and the little schoolhouse beyond. And she was walking—walking to school.

4
Visitors

The sun streamed through the window onto Mary's slender form and bandaged limb propped with fat pillows. She blinked her eyes and tossed her head from side to side. Why was she here rather than upstairs in her bedroom? And why did her leg pain so badly?

She squirmed, biting her lip as the pain shot through the injured leg. Mama tiptoed into the room and gently held her hand. Mary closed her eyes again, trying to ease the pain. Yesterday had not pained this much, not even as the doctor worked to remove the limb.

Through the opened window she heard the tap of a hammer. What could anyone be hammering so early this morning? This horrible pain! Where was relief?

Light footsteps crossed the floor and Mary turned to see Maggie coming with a cup and saucer. The steam curled upwards as Maggie stooped by her side.

"Are you hungry?" Maggie asked.

"Not really."

"I wish I had something more for your breakfast, but the doctor said you cannot have anything but liquids for awhile," said Maggie.

Mama rearranged Mary and the pillows in a comfortable sitting position and handed her the cup. She sipped at it and set the cup down. She squeezed her eyes shut tightly. When would this pain go away? When would this all pass so she could get up and run as she always had?

A clatter at the entrance broke into her thoughts. Coming towards her was Dr. Turner with an eyebrow raised and a slight smile on his lips.

"How are you doing?" he asked, pulling a chair to her side.

Her blue eyes gazed ahead and she said dreamily, "It hurts a lot, but I'll manage."

"Let me take a look and see how the leg is doing," Doctor Turner said.

She tried to smile in spite of the pain as the doctor examined and redressed her leg. She sucked in her breath and bit her lip as the tears threatened. Such pain! She blinked hard to hold back the tears that brimmed on her lower eyelids. At last the redressing was complete. She squirmed comfortably into her pillows and drew a deep, jerky sigh.

"You are very brave, Mary," said Doctor Turner.

"How is she doing?" Mama asked.

"As good as can be expected," he answered. "Time and rest are very important here. See you tomorrow. Take care of yourself."

Mary watched him cross the room and exit the door. What a kind, patient doctor he had been. She looked up and saw Papa and a neighbor, George Shifflet, crossing the room. She knew George's children, especially Stella who was her age. She looked forward to going to school with Stella and all the other Shifflet children.

"Good morning, Mary," said Mr. Shifflet, extending his hand for a handshake.

"Good morning," Mary responded, placing her hand in the large one. "How is Stella?"

"She is doing fine, thank you."

"I am anxious to see her again," said Mary.

"Maybe she can come visit you," offered Papa.

"That would be good!" exclaimed Mary.

"All right. I'll tell her you would enjoy a visit."

"Thank you," Mary smiled faintly in spite of the pain throbbing in her stump. "Did I hear you hammering something, Papa?"

"Yes, Dear."

"What are you making, Papa?"

"A box."

"What is the box for?" she asked.

Papa cleared his throat and paused. "For your foot and leg," he answered.

"Are you going to bury it, Papa?"

"Either George or I will. Your foot and limb cannot be useful any longer."

Papa glanced around to find Mama. "I need some white cloth to line the box," he said.

Mama rose quickly, without a word, and headed toward the cupboard of dress fabric. In a short while she was back and handed Papa the white material.

Papa stroked Mary's hair gently, then quietly spun on his heels and walked out with George

Shifflet.

The stump throbbed with pain. Mary looked down at the fat bandage while tears stole down her cheeks. Why did this have to happen? Why all the pain? How could she possibly walk to school with her sisters and brothers and the Shifflet neighbors? When, oh when, would things be righted?

She heard Mama chatting with someone at the door. Soon the visitors came into the room and stood before her gazing at her in pity. She wished they would not look at her so. She stretched out her hand in greeting and smiled weakly.

For many days this was to be customary—the arrival of many concerned family, friends, ministers, relatives, and neighbors. Bashful children stared in wonder at her fat bandage and shortened leg. Mary especially enjoyed the visits of little girls, Naomi Koogler, Vera Early, Stella Shifflet, Mollie Flemings, Myrtie Knicely, and others. Their girlish chatter and giggles brightened her days and lightened her heart.

The visitors brought sunny thoughts and wishes to Mary and her family. Many carried dishes of food for her family but she could not taste any. Once in awhile, someone handed her a small gift. Most of all, the presence of loved ones helped to ease the pain and brighten a lengthy recovery.

At times the pain increased so greatly that she could do nothing but cry. Even a gift or the hand of a tiny visitor could not ease that kind of pain. Tears streamed down her face while solemn faces bowed in prayer.

"My dear little Mary. How you must suffer," sobbed Mother. "If only you could be relieved of pain and walk again."

"Now, now," Papa comforted, placing his strong hands on Mama's shoulder. "I have a plan. When Mary is able, I will take her to Washington, D.C., where they make artificial legs for people."

"Shall we sing for Mary?" someone suggested.

Then Papa gathered her in his strong arms and paced the floor in rhythm with the hymn. While hymns rose, an angel hovered unseen in the room. An angel, her Papa, family, and friends who sang helped to comfort and ease the pain.

A tear clung to her eyelid as another song was sung. Back and forth Papa paced, cradling her in his strong arms. Her eyelids drooped. Another song, another tear and she lay limp in Papa's arms, fast asleep.

5

Pink Pudding

The teakettle lid rattled in the kitchen under the pressure of boiling water. Aunt Mattie poured coffee in the china cups and passed them to the visiting friends. A platter of sweets was served and sampled as the men and ladies visited and cheered Mary.

For several days she had had nothing but liquid—tea, juice, broth, and the like. She heard the clatter of platters and bowls of food visitors placed on the table in the kitchen.

She placed her hand on her stomach, feeling a growl coming on. Aunt Mattie, who had come home to help since the injury, trudged up to Mary with a steaming cup of soup. Why could it not be something more tasty?

Dr. Turner made his regular visit every day, watching the healing process and encouraging her in every way. One day after he had redressed the leg, he sat down and breathed a deep sigh.

"I'm very pleased with the healing, Mary. You are doing very well."

"Thank you, Doctor Turner," she said, her blue eyes sparkling as a giggle escaped. "And you are a good doctor."

"Thank you. Do you have any questions before I go?"

She blinked back brightly. "Yes I have, Doctor Turner. When may I eat?"

"Well now, let me see. It has been several days. Are you hungry?"

"Sure am."

"Fine. Hunger is a good sign, a mighty good sign." He turned to Mama. "Mary may have something soft to eat today."

"Something soft. Hum-m-m," Mama mused. "Let me see what is in the kitchen."

Mama's long skirts swished past her as the doctor gathered his hat and bag. Mary watched his tall slender figure stride across the room. He turned at the doorway and nodded.

"Good day, Miss Mary. Keep improving."

She giggled and waved, then sat up as Mama stepped into the room with a saucer. Mary stared at the saucer. Could it really be pink tapioca pudding? Mama sat the saucer on her lap and Mary scooped up a big bite immediately. The pink pudding spread over her tongue and slipped down her throat. She scooped up another spoonful and another and another.

"Slow down, Mary," Mama chuckled.

"M-m-m. Pink pudding," said Mary, closing her eyes and savoring the flavor. She opened her eyes. "It's good!"

Quickly she cleaned the plate and held it out to Mama for a refill.

"Not too much at once, Mary," Mama said, smiling happily. "My, I'm glad to see you improving."

But Mary was not listening. She was licking every bit of pink pudding from the spoon and saucer.

6

Helpers

Mary scooted to the edge of the couch, letting her limb extend over the side. She plopped her gloomy face into her hands and pushed her elbows into her knees. The pain had gradually subsided as time passed. Now what was there to do?

She had learned to scoot around on the floor and play with Baby Mabel and younger children. At least that was a change from her usual place on the sofa.

Many people had come to visit, to cheer and encourage. She loved the company, but life on the sofa seemed lifeless! Would she ever be able to walk again, to play tag with the other children? How was she ever to keep up with the children when she walked to school with them? If only she could walk again.

"You surely are improving," Mama said, fluffing the pillows surrounding her. "You aren't hurting so much anymore."

Mary did not answer. She waited until Mama finished arranging the pillows, then plopped her chin back into the palms of her hands.

Aunt Mattie swished through the living room with the watering can, stopping suddenly before her. "May I get your doll for you?" she asked.

Mary shook her head without changing her position.

"Here," said Mama, pulling little Mabel to the couch, "play with Mabel. She'll cheer you up."

Mary heard a knock at the door as Mama fluffed the last pillow. Aunt Mattie watered a plant, then hurried to the door.

"Hello," she said. "Come in. Mary, Ben Southerly is here to see you."

Mary sat upright, a faint smile crossing her face as the man approached. So many friends and neighbors had come. Was he just another curious visitor?

"I brought you something," Mr. Southerly smiled kindly. "I made these just for you." He held out crutches just the right size. "See, use them like this." He demonstrated how to swing between the crutches.

Mary scooted off the couch and placed the homemade crutches under her arms. How was it done?

"Like this?"

"That's right. Now swing a bit forward," said Mr. Southerly.

She allowed her weight to shift onto the crutches as she swung forward. Her foot just touched the floor when she lost her balance and tumbled in a heap on the floor.

"Are you all right?" Mama asked, helping her to her feet.

"Yes, just fine," Mary answered. "I'll try again."

She concentrated hard, allowing her body weight

to shift to the crutches momentarily until her foot was anchored to the floor. She gave the floor a little push with her foot and swung forward a bit shakily.

"Keep trying," her family encouraged.

"Try again."

In a little while she had the idea.

"Look at Mary go!" her brothers and sisters cried as they trailed behind her wherever she went.

Breathless from the exercise, Mary looked up to see Papa standing by Mama watching the performance. Both of their smiles faded the lines that had been etched in their foreheads for weeks since the accident. They even chuckled a bit seeing her spryness come to life again.

One day a clatter in the driveway aroused Mary's attention. From the window she saw Aunt Mattie arriving in the buggy with a funny looking contraption. Brothers and sisters left varied duties to investigate what Aunt Mattie was bringing home. Mary hobbled outside on her crutches and stood leaning on them. What was that thing with wheels?

Was Aunt Mattie bringing a wagon for frolicking children to ride down the barn bank? Maybe Aunt Mattie had purchased a cart to use in her garden and flower beds. Or was this something to add to Aunt Mattie's many items she collected?

Mary trembled with excitement as Aunt Mattie walked around the buggy and lifted the "thing" down to the ground.

Aunt Mattie was smiling as she rolled the carriage toward her. She saw her brothers and sisters bounce along behind Aunt Mattie, popping questions all the while.

"What is it, Aunt Mattie?"

"I'll show you," Aunt Mattie said. "I brought you something, Mary. Here sit in it and I'll give you a ride."

Why, it was a wheelchair—just right for herself!

She eased herself onto the seat while Aunt Mattie lay the crutches away. She felt the bump, bump of rough driveway as Aunt Mattie strode across the yard and driveway. Behind her she heard the children frolicking in excitement, blending in with her own laughter. And there was Grandmother peering with interest from the doorway.

"Now you can go on long rides and enjoy the countryside," said Grandmother.

"This is exciting-g-g," sang Mary as the brothers and sisters clamored nearby to give her rides.

Aunt Mattie smiled at their pleasure, gathered up the crutches, and hurried to the kitchen for her regular cup of coffee.

Summer gave way to fall. Mama packed school lunches and waved good-bye to her children. Mary watched from the window as Annie, Ellie, and John scampered toward the river basin to the east. She watched until the figures faded in the distance. Would she some day be able to run along with them swinging her lunch pail on her way to school? Would God provide a way for her to walk again?

On September 16, 1908, exciting news came. Henry and Bertie had a wee baby girl, Arline. Mary shivered with excitement. She was an aunt at five years old!

Sometime later, she was able to hold the tiny pink bundle. She fingered the bitty fingers—Henry's own little baby, her own little niece.

Fall days chilled into November, then December. Now frost had grown around the window panes overnight. Mary scratched a spot clear in the frost to watch her brothers and sisters walk to school. Through the peephole she watched them until they disappeared among the gray trees along the river. She felt a hand on her shoulder and turned to see Papa who squatted beside her.

"I have a plan, Mary. You and I are going to Washington, D.C. There a man will prepare you a wooden leg so you can walk without crutches."

"Really?"

"Would you like that?"

"Very much, Papa."

"Then we will go."

"Just you and me, Papa?"

"Just you and me," Papa said as a great smile crept up his cheeks.

7
To Washington, D.C.

Chug-a-chug-a-chug. The train sped nearer and nearer to Washington, D.C. Mary looked at Papa, tall and strong, beside her. What a kind and good Papa she had, taking her to Washington, D.C., for a new leg. Chug-a-chug-a-chug. Too-ooo-ott. She watched tall buildings speeding past her window. What would it be like in Washington, D.C.? It did not matter for Papa was near her in this strange city. What would the new leg be like she wondered. Would she be able to run and play without crutches?

"We are almost there, Mary," Papa leaned over and whispered. "Now you be my big brave girl."

"I will, Papa," she whispered back.

Tooo-oo-ooot. Chug-a-chug-a-chug. Too-oo-oot.

"D.C. ahead. D.C. ahead," the conductor called.

Mary clasped her bag closely and reached for the crutches. She noticed Papa fingering his black hat nervously. At last the train stopped. Papa assisted her down the steps and peered into the crowd ahead. She looked up at Papa but he was searching among

"D.C. ahead," the conductor called.

the baggage for the wheelchair and luggage. At last it was located among the shuffle of the crowd. She slipped into the seat of the wheelchair and held her crutches as Papa rolled her along through the crowd of people.

"How many people!" Mary exclaimed.

"Yes, there are a lot of people," agreed Papa. "Washington, D.C., is a big city."

"Someone is calling your name, Papa."

"Harmon Whitmore! Hello!" Papa spoke as he extended a hand in greeting.

"Good to see you," Mr. Whitmore said. He stooped to shake Mary's hand. "Do you remember when my family lived in your community?"

Mary's head dropped immediately when she realized he was speaking to her. "Yes, sir," she nodded.

"Your ride is this way," Mr. Whitmore said, patting her hand and drawing her mind back to the present.

Papa pushed her in the wheelchair on the busy sidewalk until they reached Mr. Whitmore's buggy.

"Well, Mary, we are here," Papa said.

While Mr. Whitmore untied the horse, Papa placed her on the seat and tucked a blanket around her. Then he folded the wheelchair and placed it in the back of the buggy. Papa leaped up into the buggy beside her. Soon the horse trotted away carrying them into the big city.

She looked up at Papa and he smiled down at her. She need not be afraid in this strange big city. Her kind Papa was with her, but more than that the heavenly Father was watching over her also.

She sat forward on the seat watching unfamiliar scenes. "Look!" Mary called, calling attention to Papa. "Ladies are bicycling on the streets."

"That is considered quite fashionable for Washington, D.C.," said Mr. Whitmore. "Smooth pavements make riding enjoyable for the ladies. It is quite in style to have elaborate biking uniforms such as you see."

"These paved roads are quite a contrast to our unpaved roads back home," chuckled Papa.

The buggy moved on, passing strange sights. There was the marketplace where rich and poor alike mingled on the sidewalk buying from the local merchants. Just then a clatter ahead caught her attention.

"Look, Papa," she said, pointing at the object approaching.

"That is a motor car, Mary," said Papa.

"It's hard to believe they can go by themselves," said Mary.

"We will likely see a few motor cars in Washington, D.C.," Papa said.

"We do not have them at home, Papa."

"No, we don't. They are very expensive. Most are used in big cities by rich people."

She giggled as the automobile chugged, snorted, and popped as it passed. She waved but the frustrated driver pressed his head forward, keeping the vehicle going.

At that moment, Mr. Whitmore pointed ahead.

"There's the White House. That's where President Roosevelt and Princess Alice live," he said.

"The President, Papa?" Mary asked.

"Yes. At this very moment President Roosevelt may be making some very important decisions," said Papa.

"Who is Princess Alice?" Mary asked.

"She is the daughter of President Roosevelt. Her mother died when she was a baby," Mr. Whitmore answered.

"Poor girl," said Mary sadly.

"President Roosevelt married another lady later," said Papa. "Mrs. Roosevelt and the President have four other children. Princess Alice is well cared for in the White House."

"Here we are," Mr. Whitmore said, slowing the horse. "Whoa!"

The buggy came to a standstill. Papa hopped out, stretched out a hand to help her down, and handed her the crutches. She swung herself between the crutches and looked toward the house. In the window she saw the faces of a boy and a girl. She halted a moment and waved at them. The girl waved back, but the boy did not wave at all.

Papa picked her up, crutches and all, and whisked her up the stairs into the warmth of the Whitmore house.

8

The Big City

"Come on in. Welcome to our home," Mrs. Whitmore said.

Papa set Mary down and removed her coat and cap.

"Just make yourselves comfortable," continued Mrs. Whitmore. "It is so cold out there. How about a cup of tea?"

"That would be fine," Papa answered, placing Mary's coat and cap and his black hat on the coat rack by the front door.

Sweet fragrance drifted from Mrs. Whitmore as she spun around and walked toward the kitchen. Mrs. Whitmore's fashionable skirts and hair seemed stylish compared to the attire of country women where Mary lived.

A young boy stole sheepishly into the room and stared at Mary's leg. She squirmed uneasily. The friendly little girl sauntered up to her and placed a doll in her lap.

Mary smiled bashfully. The little girl, Thelma,

smiled back. In a short while Thelma had become her friend as they sipped hot tea together from pretty teacups. They chattered to each other while Papa and Mr. Whitmore discussed grown-up topics.

As evening darkened, Mary's eyes became too heavy to notice the young boy's dislike of her.

Mary in the big city.

"Mr. Rohrer, let me show you your beds. I see Mary is very tired," Mrs. Whitmore said.

Papa helped Mary into her nightgown. After prayers, Papa's strong arms carefully placed her between the clean sheets. Even as she closed her eyes she prayed, "Help the people at the factory to make a proper leg for me. Help me to walk again . . ."

The next morning arrived so soon. She opened her eyes and sat up in the strange bed. Today was the day she and Papa would go to the factory. What would it be like at the factory? What was a wooden leg like?

"Are you awake already, Mary?" Papa asked.

"Yes, Papa, What an exciting day!"

"Let me help you get dressed. Mrs. Whitmore has breakfast almost ready, then we will be off to the factory."

When Mary had her stomach filled, Papa helped her into her coat and cap. She clasped the crutches and eagerly sped to the front door.

"I'm ready, Papa," she said.

"So am I," he answered. Then turning to Mrs. Whitmore he said, "Thank you for the beds and food. We will be back this evening."

Outdoors, Papa helped Mary into the little wheel-chair and pushed her forward, down the walkway, and onto the sidewalk beside the busy street.

Mary gazed at all the city sites as Papa turned corner after corner. Horses trotted past taking elegant ladies and gentlemen on some social call.

"We are almost at the factory now," Papa said looking ahead.

"Papa, here comes another motor car!"

A fine gentleman crossed the street nearby, but Mary watched the motor car as it sputtered and jerked. It sputtered again, then came to a standstill. Mary smothered a giggle as she watched the driver hop out and stomp to the front of the car.

"He's pretty angry," said Papa laughing. There's a fellow in the horse and buggy stopping to help him. Sometimes the old ways are still the best."

"I would not like to part with ol' Pet," said Mary.

"I should say not," replied Papa.

The rustle of a lady's skirt caught Mary's attention. She gazed in awe at the lady in elegant silk with hands buried in a fur muff. The lady peered down at her and eyed Papa curiously.

Mary looked down at her own plain garb, then back to the lady. The lady lifted her nose into the air and swished past her and Papa.

"I think," said Papa, with a quirk at the corner of his mouth, "that the country is the best place for you and me."

"I think so too," said Mary.

"Well, here is the factory. Let's go in and see what they can do for you, Mary."

9
At The Factory

"Hello," Papa greeted the strange man just inside the factory.

"Good morning, Mr. Rohrer?"

"That's correct."

"And you are Mary?" the man asked, extending a hand of greeting.

"Yes, sir," she answered bashfully.

"I'm Mr. Hanger. Welcome to our factory. Please be seated," he said, motioning to nearby chairs.

"Thank you," said Papa helping Mary remove her coat and cap and assisting her into a comfortable chair.

"I know you are anxious for a new leg, Mary," said Mr. Hanger. "We will be taking measurements today to make a leg that fits you just right. But before doing that I want to tell you a story. Do you like stories?"

She nodded her head eagerly.

"During the Civil War, a young man named James was wounded in battle. His leg was so injured the doctor had to remove his leg. After his leg healed, he went home and asked to be left alone in his room upstairs. No one was to enter his room for any purpose."

Mary listened as the kind man told the story. What could James be doing upstairs in his room all to himself? Could he be pitying himself? Mr. Hanger continued the story.

"Young James asked for supplies to use in his room. He asked for lumber, barrel staves and wood from willow trees near his home.

"Upstairs in his room the young man worked and whittled for three months. After all his hard work, he walked downstairs and surprised his family with a new wooden leg. From then on, James Edward Hanger spent his entire life making artificial limbs for others."

"Your name is Hanger," said Papa when the story was finished. "Is he a relative of yours?"

"He is my relative," Mr. Hanger confirmed. He walked over to a counter and drew out a strange looking leg. "This is what your leg will look like, Mary."

She stared at the leg. It did look like a leg.

"It can move and bend at the joints almost like your leg. James Edward Hanger worked a long time to make a leg that worked well."

Slowly she reached out her hand to finger the model leg.

"Here is where you will fasten the limb to your leg," Mr. Hanger said.

Skillfully he slipped a soft stocking over her stump and slid the artificial limb in place. Then he laced it snugly in place.

"There," he quipped, "only yours will fit much better. After awhile you can be off on the run."

She looked up at Mr. Hanger, then at Papa. A faint smile increased to a wide grin across her face.

"And now I want to measure your leg. Measuring will not be painful. Shall we get started?"

She nodded.

Mr. Hanger measured her leg this way and that way, jotting down the measurements. After a time he sat down.

"That will be all for today," he said looking from Mary to Papa. "I would like you to return tomorrow for a fitting."

"Certainly," said Papa. "We will be glad to do that as we are staying nearby.

"Good," said the man. "I'll see you tomorrow then. Good-bye, Mary," he said stooping to shake her hand. Then standing up he shook Papa's hand. "Good-bye, Mr. Rohrer."

"Good-bye," said Papa.

"Good-bye," said Mary smiling with excitement. "I can hardly wait for my new limb, Mr. Hanger."

10
Papa's Gift

There was time to sightsee in Washington, D.C., while waiting for the leg to be manufactured. Between visits to the factory, Papa wheeled Mary to many interesting places in the unfamiliar city.

"I'm certainly glad for this wheelchair," Papa said. "You would get mighty tired trying to walk all these blocks on crutches."

"Yes, Papa," Mary replied. "But why did some people not want my wheelchair to come inside their building?"

"They thought the wheels might damage the floors," answered Papa. "But once they saw the soft rubber around the wheels, they didn't object."

"Papa, may we look at the toys in this store?" she asked as they passed a window displaying many toys.

"Let me see," Papa said drawing out his watch. "Hm-m-m. I believe we do have time before the evening meal at the Whitmores."

Up and down the aisles Papa pushed her in the

wheelchair.

"Look at all the toys!" she exclaimed.

"I've never seen so many myself, Mary. This is quite a big toy store."

"Look at that cute bear, Papa!"

Papa picked up the bear, inspected it, and handed it to her. She smiled as she moved the furry legs and arms. Likely not a cousin or relative back home owned such an adorable toy.

"May I help you?" a friendly voice asked.

"We are just looking," answered Papa.

The man spied her in the wheelchair. For a moment he looked at her leg, then politely turned his attention to the bear in her hands.

"This is a Steiff bear," the clerk explained. "A lady in Germany named Margaret Steiff makes these bears." The clerk eyed her in the wheelchair, smiled, and went on. "Both of Miss Steiff's legs became paralyzed because of polio."

Mary perked her head listening. So the maker of this toy also knew about a wheelchair! And could not walk at all! She looked at Papa. He was listening with interest.

"Miss Steiff made toys to give away. She made them from felt scraps from a nearby factory. People liked her toys and asked for them so often she decided to make them to sell. Sometimes Miss Steiff invited children to her home where she entertained them with a tea party and stories."

Mary glanced at her special bear then up at the clerk with a smile.

The clerk continued, "The children loved the story best of *Goldilocks and the Three Bears*. Around

1903 she decided to make a toy bear. In her own kitchen she cut the pieces and sewed them together by hand."

Mary turned the limbs on the bear, listening as the clerk talked. She noticed Papa was listening carefully.

"Toy bears became popular about two years ago in 1906. Our President, Theodore Roosevelt, is a great hunter. On one hunting trip when he had shot nothing, his aides captured a bear for him to shoot. This was to show the United States the President's successful hunt."

Mary noticed Papa nodding his head and smiling as he recognized the story.

"The President chased the bear away because his tender heart couldn't shoot it," Papa said chuckling.

"That's right," agreed the clerk.

Mary stroked the soft fur of the toy bear thinking how fortunate that a bear had escaped a kill because of the President's kindness.

The clerk continued, "One day the President had a very fine dinner in the White House. The tables were decorated with many bears dressed in hunter and fishermen outfits. Someone asked, "What kind of bears are these?" Another responded, "They are Teddie's bears."

"What did he mean—Teddie's bears?" Mary asked, looking from Papa to the clerk, who was chuckling over the story.

"Teddy is a nickname for our President, Theodore Roosevelt," said the clerk.

"From then on toy bears were called teddy bears?" Mary asked.

"That's right," answered the clerk.

"It is proper though to address our President as President Theodore Roosevelt," said Papa.

"Yes, Papa."

"Since that dinner in the White House, two years ago, millions of teddy bears have been sold," said the clerk.

Mary turned the little bear over. A squeak escaped from the toy.

"Yes, he squeaks too," chuckled the clerk.

"Do you like the bear, Mary?" Papa asked.

"Oh yes!"

"Then he shall be yours," Papa said, wheeling the wheelchair up to the counter.

"Really, Papa?"

"Yes," he chuckled, "your very own."

Mary's eyes sparkled as Papa paid for the bear, then placed it into her arms.

"There, it's yours now."

She beamed at Papa and waved good-bye to the clerk as Papa wheeled her away. Hugging her new bear tightly, she scooted to a more comfortable position as Papa headed her toward the Whitmore's. She scarcely noticed the activity on the streets and sidewalks. Instead she squeaked the bear and giggled in delight.

Such was her joy as Papa pushed her wheelchair into the Whitmore's walkway. She caught sight of Alden's mischievous face peering out the window at her. Soon she and Papa had left the busy streets and the chilly December air behind for the warmth of house and friendship. There she and Thelma, a kind, considerate playmate, would spend the remaining hours playing together. Alden, however, watched from the sidelines, sometimes grinning, sometimes glaring. She wondered if he disliked her or if he was jealous of her new toy. Or did he find her missing limb an advantage for sport? She did not know.

One morning while Papa read the morning paper, Mary wandered into the kitchen for a drink. Alden slipped into the kitchen behind her just as Mrs. Whitmore stepped out of the room. Flour, eggs, and butter surrounded the bowl on the table where Mrs. Whitmore was baking a cake.

Mary balanced herself between the crutches holding her precious bear in one hand and sipping from a cup with the other. She had just placed the empty cup on the table when Alden scooped up a handful of flour and threw it directly at her.

She squeezed her eyes shut to resist the sting of flour in her eyes. She felt herself tottering and spread her crutches outward to balance herself. When she opened her eyes, she found she was stable. Her bear had fallen to the floor. And Alden was gone. That boy! She giggled and dusted herself off, picked up the bear, and went in search of Thelma.

Her bear had fallen to the floor.

11

A New Leg

The days in Washington, D.C., sped by. The Hanger factory had the necessary measurements and fittings to craft her artificial limb. Now she and Papa were homeward bound.

Mary clutched her new Steiff teddy bear and watched the familiar countryside whiz past the windows. She was thinking about the new leg that would come to the house by mail. The new leg would replace those crutches Ben Southerly gave her and would help her be like other boys and girls.

Chug-a-chug. Too-oott. Too-oott. How good it would be to be home again.

"Dayton ahead," the conductor interrupted her thinking. "Please stay seated until the coach has stopped."

Papa stirred restlessly. "Almost home, little gal," he chuckled, "and shortly that new leg will be shipped to you straight from Washington, D.C."

"I'm going to walk just as good as ever, Papa," she said smiling up at him.

"I hope so," he replied with a doubtful twinkle in his eye.

"I will. You just wait and see."

Too-oo-oott. Chug-a-chug. The train slowed as the Dayton town limits came into view.

"Passengers leaving the coach, please watch your step," the conductor called.

She gathered her crutches and moved nimbly down the aisle. At the steps Papa swept her, crutches and all, down the steps and onto the ground at the familiar Dayton depot. There was Henry in the buggy waiting nearby to take them home.

The last miles seemed long even though the horse kept up a good pace. Closer and closer she came to home. Up Dry River Road she and Papa and Henry rode and into the driveway. There stood the family pressing eager faces against Mama's clean windows.

Papa stepped down from the buggy, then assisted her out of the buggy, and handed her the crutches. A gust of north air whipped at her but she pressed on to the house. Up the stairs she climbed with Papa following behind. The door burst open and there was Mama with outstretched arms welcoming them home. Her brothers and sisters stared at her leg.

"But she doesn't have a new leg."

"It will come someday soon in a big box from Washington, D.C.," explained Papa.

"What will it look like?"

"It will look almost like her own leg, only this one will be wooden."

"Will she walk with a wooden leg?"

Papa nodded. "Yes, she should walk almost as normal as before."

Mary quickly told about the factory. "I'm going to walk without crutches," she said happily.

Days slipped by and chores and schedules followed regularly. Smoke spiraled from the Rohrer house as the chilly days of December passed on one by one. Christmas days were spent enjoying friends and relatives around long tables of prepared food.

Then one day, just after Christmas, the big box arrived.

"It's here! It's here, Mary!" John exclaimed.

"What's here?" she asked.

"Your leg is here!"

Nimbly she maneuvered herself by crutches to the window to watch the mailman. She hurried over to the door as the big box was shoved inside. The postman smiled, then waved at the eager family, and hurried away.

"Can we open it, Papa?" the eager boys clamored.

"Since this box is for Mary, how about letting her open it?" said Papa.

"Hurry and open it, Mary," the children urged.

All the family, including Aunt Mattie and Grand-mother, crowded around to watch. One flap was opened. Then two. Three. And four. She pulled out the smooth-finished wooden leg.

"Try it on, Mary! Let's see you walk!"

Papa stooped to pull the soft sock onto her stump as they had been shown in Washington. He slipped the wooden leg over the stocking and tied the arti-ficial limb in place.

"Her other sock and shoe!" Mama exclaimed dashing upstairs for the sock and shoe which had been put away for months.

Soon the lesser worn shoe and sock were on and Papa pulled her to a standing position. She let loose of Papa and balanced herself. She took a step. The wooden leg felt strange fastened at the end of her stump, but it held her up. She took another step, feeling Papa's presence to catch her if she were to fall. She felt wobbly and uncertain, but she was standing—and walking—without crutches! She would walk. She would!

Maggie and Annie, with the young, cheered her on. Aunt Mattie, Grandmother, and Mama wiped their eyes as happy tears gathered.

"That's the best Christmas present I could have had, Papa," said Mary smiling brightly at him.

Papa winked at her, then walked to the porch and took his hat from its peg.

"Gotta get the barn work done," he said to the family.

He stepped outside and burst into a lusty hymn.

12

Adjustments

Winter temperatures plunged below zero and remained there for some days and nights. Each night the ice on ponds, creeks, and rivers thickened until the neighborhood knew it was time for ice skating. From attics children, youth, men, and women collected their ice clamps, bundled warmly, and made their way to the icy surfaces. A fire glowed nearby to warm chilled toes and fingers between the graceful performances.

Mary stood near the fire watching the skaters. There were Maggie and her older brothers and sisters, gliding across the ice in graceful strides. They skimmed and twirled individually or raced after each other in a tag game. Sometimes they misjudged a step or turn which resulted in a sprawled heap scooting across the glossy surface. Mary giggled at their displays.

A blast of crisp, north air struck her full force from behind, almost sweeping her off her feet. Br-r-r. She braced herself, planting the wooden limb squarely in place, and shoving her other foot closer to the embers to warm the toes.

The fire toasted her toes, cheeks, and fingers until she was cozy-warm. If only she could put on ice clamps and skim across the ice too. She looked down at her wooden limb. No, the ice was too risky. Papa had said one fall could easily break the specially crafted wooden limb.

She glanced out at the skaters again as reality sunk into her mind. She would probably never be able to skate on ice like others. Never. She bit her lip to still its quivering.

"Heh," a voice caught her attention.

She swallowed hard at the lump in her throat and turned to see Amos skating towards her with a sled.

"Want a ride, Mary? Come on! I'll give you a really good one," he said.

Her eyes brightened and a grin revealed her white teeth. Amos held out his hand and helped steady her on the slippery ice until she was seated on the sled.

"Hang on tight," Amos called to her.

Then away she skimmed behind Amos, whizzing past the skaters. She giggled as he pulled her this way and that. The other children skated alongside and cheered for her. Happily Mary cheered too as she watched the flash of Amos' skates cut into the ice. Suddenly he planted his sharp pointed blades deep into the glossy surface and pulled firmly on the sled ropes. Mary felt the sled lurch forward with extra speed so she hung on tightly. The sled skidded in a wide circle around Amos and coasted to a stop in front of him. She looked up at Amos whose breath puffed warm steam into the frosty air when he

Away she skimmed behind Amos . . .

laughed.

"Was it fun, Mary?" he asked.

"Fun? I'll say it was!" she giggled.

"Let me take her for a ride," said William.

"I want a turn too," said John.

Now she too could have fun on the ice. As winter advanced and snow fell, she joined the family for sleigh rides and coasting. Little by little, she learned new freedoms which allowed her to enter into the life of work and play with her family. Mary was enjoying her new freedom when the unexpected happened.

One day she noticed her stump ached. She tried to ignore it but the pain continued. Sitting down, she unlaced the artificial limb, pulled off the stocking and examined where the pain radiated. Why, no wonder!

"Mama, come and look at my stump," she called toward the kitchen where Mama was busy.

Mama's skirts and apron swished against the

doorway as she hurried in to examine the leg.

"Why, Mary! There are blisters forming on your stump. You'll need to take it easy for awhile until those places heal."

"Aw-w-w. You mean I can't walk, Mama?"

"Just for a while. Your stump is still getting used to the wooden leg. In time you will have less problem with blisters."

"Aw-w-w, Mama."

"You have really been using that limb. Here, let me put some ointment on those places and bandage your stump so it can heal."

While she rested and healed, she helped Maggie and Mama roll the carpet rags into large balls for making rugs. And she even used her crutches again. Someday she would be free of the crutches for good!

13
Grandmother

Sunlight streamed through the windows of Mary's room in spite of chilling January temperatures. Shivering, Mary sat up in bed and reached for her artificial limb. How could she forget? Her stump was still too sore to use it. Sadly she lay the limb down, slid off the bed and dressed leaning against the bed for balance. Then she grabbed her crutches close by and hopped downstairs.

Papa and her brothers were just coming in from the barn early on this beautiful Sunday morning. She watched them wash in the kitchen as she slipped into her chair at the table.

Mama's Sunday best dress rustled as she passed Mary and placed the steaming food on the table. Grandmother and the older sisters moved about in the kitchen helping with the table and breakfast. And Aunt Mattie, as always, sipped her coffee from a handleless coffee cup. On a cold morning, as today, the heat from the cup warmed her hands.

"Good morning, Mary."

Mary turned to see her oldest sister, Ava, standing nearby. Ava frequently worked in other homes assisting busy mothers with children and household chores.

"Good morning, Ava. When did you get home?" Mary asked.

"Last evening after dark. Sure is good to be home. How is the stump?"

"Sore, but getting better."

"You'll soon be going strong on that leg again, won't you?" Papa said twisting her ear playfully.

"I hope so, Papa," Mary said, dodging his playful fingers by covering her ears with both arms upraised.

Papa tickled her underarms and Mary's arms came down with tremendous speed. As she doubled over with laughter, Papa tickled her ears again. Back and forth they went.

"Israel," Mama said, "Isn't that about enough teasing?"

"Enough for now," Papa said giving Mary's ear one more playful twist.

Each family member found his place at the table and prayed in their customary way—silently. Soon the family feasted on a hearty breakfast before being off to the Sunday services.

"Who will stay home from church with Grandmother and Mary today?" Papa asked when the meal was completed.

"Why can't I go to church, Papa?" Mary asked. "Please?"

"Your stump needs rest and care, Mary. Besides it is so cold you'd best stay home with Grandmother," said Papa.

Mary squeezed her faithful teddy. Someday—someday she could go to church always with her family. Papa's eyes were tender but she knew he'd say no more.

Ava piped up, "I'll stay home with Grandmother and Mary."

"It's settled then," Papa said. "You youngsters get ready for church and I'll go hitch up the horses."

Grandmother, at the ripe old age of 82, seldom attended church. Ever since Mary had known Grandmother, the only language she could speak was German, so she could not understand the English church services. Grandmother and her husband, Israel, had moved to the Shenandoah Valley in Virginia from Pennsylvania where the Mennonite people spoke German. Mary understood the language Grandmother spoke even though she could not speak nearly as fluently.

At one time Grandmother and Grandfather lived close by in a little house of their own. Since Grandfather was no longer living, Grandmother had moved into the bustling Rohrer household.

While the Rohrer family made their way in buggies to the house of worship, Mary watched Grandmother and Ava peel potatoes. They dropped the potatoes into a large kettle on the stove. At the dinner table the big family would be served a heaping dishful of mashed potatoes. In addition, there would be roast beef, vegetables and desserts which had been prepared on Saturday.

Mary turned from watching the potato process and wandered to the living room. She lay her crutches down and plopped into a soft chair. Her friendly teddy stared at her from the floor. She picked him up and turned the legs and arms. When would this stump heal so she could go to church with her family? She missed the friendly girl-chat after service.

Grandmother came into the room and sat in her rocker quietly, looking at Mary without a word. She gathered her worn Bible and slowly turned the pages. For a while she scanned the well worn pages, then placed a wrinkled finger on a verse and looked up at Mary. In German, she read and shared encouraging words of faith for the difficult times. Mary listened to the Words of Wisdom from Grandmother's Bible and felt comforted. Yes, she had come a long, long way since that fateful day in August.

The aroma of roasting beef drifted into the living room as Mary played happily. For a long while Grandmother was absorbed in the Words of Wisdom that made her life rich indeed. The sudden clatter of buggies in the driveway startled Grandmother and Mary.

"Back already?" Grandmother said as she scurried to the kitchen to whip the potatoes and check on the dinner.

Once again the family encircled the long table and chatted warmly with news from church friends and relatives. And Grandmother's tasty dinner was a wonderful Sunday contribution.

Winter activities slowed to a minimum in late January of 1909. On a Sunday afternoon, Grandmother had just visited with Preacher Gabriel Heatwole and another neighbor, Sallie Keller, who had come to call. Before night came, Grandmother suddenly slipped away into eternity.

Could it really be Grandmother had gone on? How Mary and her family would miss Grandmother reading her German Bible and her involvement with the family. Could it really be? Mary hobbled to her room as fast as her limb would allow and let the tears fall freely.

14
Spring Days

After Grandmother's passing, winter seemed to creep so slowly. Even sleigh rides and skating on the river had lost some appeal.

Through the winter months, Mary had had to adjust to her new leg. Blisters formed, healed, erupted again and healed. Gradually the stump adjusted to its wooden companion.

Mary remembered fondly of Grandmother's encouragement through those difficult months since the surgery. Grandmother had played an important part through the difficulties and adjustments.

Gradually days lengthened and snow gave way to spring rainfall which greened the meadows and the graveyard where Grandmother Rohrer was buried.

Green shoots poked through the loosened soil and burst forth with yellow blossoms across the countryside. Mountain water tumbled downstream, roaring against the sandstones in Dry River's basin. Along the river's edge fat buds on dogwood and redbud awaited longer days of sunshine to bring forth blossoms. Soon the Creator's handiwork would display white and purplish-pink throughout the tree-lined river banks.

One spring day Mary and her younger brother, Frank, entertained themselves with the pet lamb. The lamb, which had been kept on the porch, in time had become strong and frisky from loving care and leftover food.

Mary patted the lamb and held out something to eat from the slop bucket where Mama dumped table scraps. She watched Frank take his hands out of the pockets of brand-new overalls and reach into the slop bucket for something for the lamb.

"Mama doesn't want you to get those new overalls dirty," she warned Frank. "I heard her say she paid $1.89 for them."

The lamb butted playfully at her. "Stop that!" she said, giving the lamb a sound swat.

"I bet $1.89 he won't butt me," Frank said puffing out his chest daringly and jamming his hands into his pockets.

Mary watched the lamb shake his head, playfully give a leap, then back up for a running start. In a moment he charged across the porch, head down and slammed into Frank. Splat! Frank landed right in the slop bucket!

Mary clapped her hand over her mouth and snickered. Startled, Frank looked up at her as the garbage soaked into his brand-new overalls. Just then Mama peeked around the corner.

"I guess you found out what the Good Book says about pride," chuckled Mama. "There's a verse which says pride goeth before a fall."

Mary tried to hide a giggle while she and Mama pulled Frank out of the slop bucket.

"I think it's time Papa found a better place for this big lamb. Why, one this big and strong is almost a sheep!" Mama exclaimed.

Mama wiped up the thick puddles spreading on the floor under Frank's new, soggy overalls.

"Out with all of you," Mama said playfully. "Mary, you can pump water for Frank to clean up. And I'll shoo this big lamb out of here."

"May I go barefooted, Mama?" Mary asked.

"Yes, but leave the shoe on the artificial limb. Now shoo, you big lamb!" Mama flapped her apron frantically at the lamb, shooing him off the porch.

Mary squatted on the floor and hurriedly pulled off her shoe and stocking. She scrambled down the steps and out onto the new tender grass skipping like

Frank's overalls hung on the line.

a frisky spring lamb.

"There you are, Frank. Let me pump the water while you wash."

While Frank was washing, Mama came around the house with an empty bucket. "It was about time the bucket was emptied anyhow."

"Am I clean, Mama?" Frank asked.

"Better, but not clean enough. You'll need to slip out of those overalls and let me wash them."

Later that evening, Frank's overalls hung on the line, almost as crisp and new as when the price tag read $1.89.

15
Threshing

Spring days slipped by quickly and soon the children squealed with glee that school days were over until fall. Now they had time to stroll in the meadow and assist with the extra work that summer days brought. There were gardens to hoe, grass to mow, and hay to make on top of the regular chores.

In spite of the added work, summer also brought fun times. Mary and her family always enjoyed a summer day of riding to the mountains in the spring wagon. In the mountains, she and her family picnicked, hiked trails, played horseshoe, or played in the shallow river. This river was the very one which ran by her house many miles downstream.

Late in the afternoon, Mary and her family piled into the spring wagon and rode home to the chores awaiting them.

The hotter days ripened wheat fields up and down the Dry River Valley. As the wheat became golden, the threshing machine made its way into the farming community. From farm to farm the machine made its way across the community harvesting the wheat for eager farmers.

To-oo-ot, too-oot. The steam whistle from the threshing machine echoed across the Valley. Since few had telephones, the whistle signaled the end of a harvest job. By this the neighbors knew the threshing machine was moving to another location.

Too-oo-oot. Too-oo-ot. Mary and her sister Ella paused from breaking green beans into a bowl and perked sunbonneted heads in the direction of the whistle. Mary saw Mama stand up from picking beans in the garden and peer toward the sound. Papa and her brothers hustled from the barn.

"The harvest crew will be here next," Papa said, looking in the direction of the whistle sound, while raising his straw hat to scratch his head.

Mary watched Mama finish her bean row and stride to the house to check on dinner preparation. Threshing would mean a hungry crew to feed besides her large family.

Snap, snap, snap. Her bowl was filling to the top. She looked up as the threshing machine clattered into the farmyard. There were Papa and the boys running toward the machine. Soon rows of straw lay across Papa's fields. Horses and wagons followed behind with men piling straw on the wagon. Sweat rivulets rolled down the horses' sides as they pulled the wagons to the haystack by the barn.

Mary scooted from the porch swing and dashed through the kitchen door, letting it slam behind her. She placed the bowl of beans on the kitchen counter.

"Will you set the table, Mary?" Mama asked.

"Sure," Mary consented willingly. She set the

The horses . . . pulled the wagons to the haystack by the barn.

plates on the table all the while thinking of the fun they would have sliding down the haystack in the days to come.

When dinnertime arrived, the long table had been stretched even longer to accommodate the extra men. Steam curled from dishes as the men washed outside for dinner and filed into the kitchen. They shuffled to their places visiting and planning the day's work and sat down. Silence fell over the table as each anticipated prayer.

"Let us pray," Papa said.

Heads bowed. The clock on the wall ticked out the moments as inaudible prayers were lifted. When prayer was over, the dishes were passed around the table to the hungry crew. Mary watched the men eat the hearty dinner Mama had prepared. She took a bite of dinner. Yum, yum! Mama did make a good dinner!

The men scraped their platters clean, drank the water and sighed.

"That was a mighty dandy dinner, Mrs. Rohrer."

"Yes, indeed," said another. "Mighty fine dinner." When the meal was over and thanks returned, the men rose from the table and slipped out the back door.

"My," Mama said, "it sure doesn't take long to eat a meal that took several hours to fix."

Mary and Ella washed the dishes while Mama canned the beans. Mary balanced on her two legs and polished the dishes. She was so glad to be an active member of the family and do her part.

For several days the reapers harvested. Finally the whistle sounded the end of its duty on the Rohrer farm. Too-oo-ot. Papa lifted his straw hat to wave good-bye, while in the kitchen Mama put the extra dishes away and shortened the table. Mary and her siblings scampered to test their sliding ability from the top of the haystack.

Threshing brought the excitement of refilling tick mattresses. Mary helped Papa, Mama and children pull the flattened mattresses from their beds and emptied the year-old straw. Together they stuffed the mattresses full of fresh, soft straw until each was plump and round.

"Jump on the mattresses and flatten them," Mama smiled to her children.

Gleefully her brothers and sisters jumped and jumped trying to flatten and even the bulges. Mary watched from the sidelines. Would she be able to jump as she did before part of her leg was removed?

She took a step into the mattress. She jumped and tottered forward, falling into its softness. She just couldn't make that wooden limb balance on the roly poly mattresses.

She picked herself up and tried to jump. Again she fell and rolled giggling among the straw mounds. Her brother and sisters rolled too and soon the straw tick was ready for beds. When dusk approached, fluffy mattresses were placed back on the springs and fresh sheets beckoned weary workers and children.

That night Mary removed her limb, clutched her toy bear, and pulled herself up into the bouncy bed. The crickets began their night songs as the weary drifted off to sleep.

But Mary and Ella lay awake giggling as they tried to find comfortable positions in their plump bed. Gradually their giggling ceased and eyelids drooped. Mary tried to imagine the cows outside chewing their cud while the moon slowly glided above the riverbed. She knew that stars twinkled above the dark and silent Rohrer house. She was just drifting off to sleep when she heard a thud.

What was that? She was wide awake. Pulling herself to the edge of the plump mattress, she peered down at Ella on a heap on the floor. She clapped her hand over her mouth to muffle a giggle. Then Papa and Mama appeared at the door with a lamp.

"Are you hurt?" Mama asked, stooping to check on Ella.

Ella rolled slowly onto her back and began to giggle. "No, Mama," she answered. "It's just a long way from that straw tick to the floor."

Papa scooped up Ella and rolled her into bed. "You stay there and no more night tumbling," he teased.

Mary felt Ella roll against her. She giggled and Ella did too. Together they snuggled into the plump straw tick like two kittens in a haystack.

16

School

"But, Papa, I can walk to school," Mary argued, trying to persuade him to change his mind.

"I'm sorry, Mary," Papa answered, "even though school is just on the other side of the river, it is still too far for you to walk."

She pushed her teeth into her lower lip to still its trembling.

Papa continued, "I have arranged for the school-teacher to pick you up. You can ride horseback to school with him."

She blinked back the tears that were forming. In the distance through her blurred vision she could see the house where all the Shifflet children lived. Some-day she would walk with them and her sisters and brothers. Through the fields they would go, up along Dry River, over the swinging bridge, and down the road to school. But Papa said no. She felt like a dam was about to burst.

"Half a mile is just a bit much for that artificial limb, Mary," said Mama handing her the lunch pail.

"But I know I could walk it," Mary said sadly.

"Someday," Papa answered. "For now riding horseback with the schoolteacher is best."

"Here he comes on his horse," one of the children called as they skipped down the driveway on their way to school.

Mary felt Papa's strong arms encircling her waist as he swung her over the horse's back in front of the teacher.

"Take care of Mary," Papa called after them as the teacher clicked to his horse.

She felt the hair of the horse bristle against her upper legs as she adapted to the rhythm of the horse. She clutched the horse's mane as she and the teacher galloped toward the river. The horse slowed for the rocky crossing in the river. She felt the movement of muscles under her as the horse attempted to keep steady footing in the dry riverbed, then strain up the river bank. On they went on the road beside the river. Peering between the horse's ears, Mary watched the schoolhouse loom ahead.

Mary watched the schoolhouse loom ahead.

In a little, the horse slowed and stopped at the hitching post. The teacher slid off and helped her down.

Mary clasped her lunch pail and started off toward the school. Just ahead, coming her direction, was Bill Flemings. His one eye was missing and his mouth hung crooked. She knew he was a community man, but his looks frightened her.

"Well, well," said Bill, eyeing her, "so you came to school. I know who you are. You're Israel Rohrer's girl, aren't you?"

She nodded slightly and bit her lip. Clutching her lunch pail she looked around for her brother, John. The teacher had tied his horse and come up behind her.

"Don't be afraid," he said. "Bill won't hurt you. He lives down by the river where we forded."

She shook her head and smiled faintly at Bill.

"Don't mind me," Bill smiled crookedly. "They's all scared of me at first. My mouth is crooked because I ate a green persimmon."

She giggled with him, then looked up the river road where her sisters and brother with the Shifflets were entering the school grounds. There was Stella. If only she could walk to school with Stella.

Ellie took Mary's hand. "Come on, I'll help you find a place to sit," she said, trying to take care of her little sister.

"Hi," a cheery voice floated over Mary's shoulder.

Mary looked over her shoulder to see a friendly girl just older than herself.

"Hi, Mollie," Mary brightened at recognizing a neighbor.

"I hope we can be friends," Mollie smiled.

"I hope so too," Mary smiled back.

"I'll help you find a place to sit," said Mollie.

Just then Stella jogged up to her side. "You made it!" she puffed. "And you got to ride horseback!"

"I'd rather walk with you than ride horseback," sighed Mary. "Heh, we'd better get in the schoolhouse. The teacher is ringing the bell."

Mary noticed Ella was frowning. Didn't she like the new friends she had made? Now Ella was smiling and stepping aside so she, Mollie, and Stella could go ahead. Mary tipped her sunbonnet back and smiled at Stella and Mollie as they made their way up the steps with Ella just behind.

17
Two Strangers

Hoppity hop. Hoppity hop. Mary frolicked beside of her big sister Maggie one Saturday. How nice it would be to skip like she used to. However, her limb cooperated with her movements very well.

"I'm glad Mama let me walk along to the store!" Mary said. "See, I'm not tired."

"We aren't there just yet, little sister," said Maggie shifting the butter she would trade for goods at the store. "We haven't even gotten to the river yet. Then there's the swinging bridge to cross . . ."

"I know, I know," interrupted Mary, "then we get on the road, pass the school, and just beyond that is the store. I can make it."

"We'll see," said Maggie.

Mary looked at the red and golden trees spanning the riverbank. Whew! One year had passed so quickly since her accident.

"There's the swinging bridge ahead, Maggie," Mary said, stopping to wait for Maggie to catch up. "Maybe I can sit down on it before we go on."

"Are you tired?" Maggie asked. "I told you it's rather far."

"I'm a little tired, but I'll be fine if I rest."

Her feet slowed. Still she trudged on, lagging slightly behind Maggie. She watched Maggie climbing the plank up to the swinging bridge that spanned Dry River. She would catch up. It had been a long while since she had walked that bridge. Her pace quickened and soon she climbed the plank and began to make her way over the bridge. The springy motion from Maggie's weight unsteadied her, but she grasped at the sturdy cable for stability.

Now Maggie was across and the bridge stood still. Mary eased ahead, feeling the swinging bridge wobble from her weight. In the middle of the bridge she stopped and peered over the edge. Then she looked across the bridge where Maggie was waiting for her.

"Come on," Maggie said.

"You go on," Mary said, motioning toward the store. "I'll wait here and rest until you come back."

"Are you sure?"

"I'll be all right."

"I'll be back shortly," Maggie said, waving as she turned to go. Then she turned back and called, "If any bad boys come by and try to swing the bridge, you'd better get off. It'd be too bad if you slipped off the bridge into Dry River, and dry it is!"

"No one will bother me. I'll be fine."

She clung to the cable and sat down on the bridge. Breathing a deep sigh, she dangled her legs over the edge. The stump inside her artificial limb ached. Ah, she thought, this is such a peaceful place to relax.

Through the trees she could see Maggie walking briskly toward the shore. She breathed in deeply of fresh country air and swung her one leg back and forth. In her mind the wooden leg swung too, even though it actually dangled motionless over the bridge.

She pushed a pigtail over her shoulder and glanced at the puffy clouds above. A squirrel scampering onto the bridge stopped suddenly when he spied her. Quickly he spun around and sped away.

Mary laughed. Gradually the ache in her leg was easing.

"La-la-de-de-da," she sang. "La-la-de-de-da."

She stopped singing and cocked her head listening. What was that sound? Was she hearing horses? Yes, she knew she was hearing horses. She strained to see through the golden river brush and trees. There she could make out one horse. Just behind was another. Nearer the horses came until she could see two men on horseback. Who could these strangers be? She had never seen them before. She watched the horseback riders halt their horses on the riverbank. They remained seated in their saddles as they eyed the swinging bridge and spoke too softly to each other for Mary to hear.

"Heh!" one rider called to her, lifting his hat in greeting.

She stopped swinging her leg and sat up straight. "Yes," she answered.

"Think we could cross this bridge?"

Her eyes blinked in surprise. The bridge was wide enough for one person at a time to cross. Would they really try to cross it with horses?

Who could these strangers be?

The young men were waiting for an answer.

"I don't believe you better," she answered.

Suddenly the horses spun around and galloped away. Mary watched as the horseback riders sped through the trees on the road that followed the river. Above her the honk of geese distracted her from the sound of horses fading in the distance. She swung her one leg back and forth again.

Soon she saw Maggie hurrying toward her with a sack of groceries.

"Are you all right?" Maggie asked as she scrambled up the swinging bridge.

"Just fine," said Mary. "I'm rested now."

"What did those fellows want?" Maggie asked, breathless from running.

"They wanted to cross this swinging bridge," giggled Mary.

"Silly fellows!" Maggie exclaimed, giving Mary a hand and pulling her to a standing position. "And you scared them away?"

"I just told them I didn't think they better. And they listened!"

Two voices blended into laughter as they headed homeward. In the west Mary and her sister watched the Master Painter's unseen brush blend golden streaks into pink and red beauty above the mountain ridge. Mary gazed with awe at the scene before her. Then she realized Maggie was nudging her elbow to get her attention.

"Do you know Alta Baugher who lives near the store?"

"Yes, she's four or five, I believe," Mary said.

"Well, Alta is very sick."

"Doth not he see my ways, and count all my steps?" (Job 31:4). A swinging bridge similar to the one Mary crossed in her young days.

"What's wrong?"

"They don't know," Maggie responded sadly. "We ought to pray earnestly for her life."

"Is she really sick enough to die?" Mary asked.

"Yes. I was asked to see if Ella, our sister, could come and stay with Alta tonight. Mary Showalter is also going to stay the night at the Baughers."

They were almost home. Mary watched the reds fade into grays and navys. She prayed silently for Alta. Surely He would hear and spare her life, would He not?

18

A Difficult Duty

In spite of the prayers offered on Alta Baugher's behalf, sad news came the next morning. Little Alta had departed this life.

Mary pushed her food round and round on her breakfast plate. She wondered where Alta was now that she no longer was alive. And why did God not answer the prayers to help Alta get well?

Poor little Alta had had infantile paralysis.* Little by little she had declined in health until now. Now she was gone. If she had lived, Alta would have been crippled all her life.

Under the table, Mary fingered her leg. She could feel the laces on her wooden leg under her dress and petticoat. Certainly, she had come a long way from the night of the operation. Within herself a sense of thankfulness swelled for God's blessing of healing. But what about Alta?

Mary glanced around the table and noticed Ella's

---

*Today we would call it polio.

place was empty. Yes, Ella had stayed the night to comfort and help Alta and the big family. Mary took another bite of food. No one spoke much this morning. She was glad when breakfast was over and other activities of the day began. Later that day someone stopped at the house to talk to Mary.

"The Baughers want you to be a pallbearer at Alta's funeral."

"Me?" Mary asked.

"Yes. Do you think you could do that with a wooden leg?"

"Not by myself, surely," said Mary.

"No, there will be three other girls to help you. Mary Rhodes, Stella Shifflett, and Myrtie Knicely will also be pallbearers.

Mary fingered her wooden leg. Would it be strong enough? Could she really help carry Alta's casket? The Baughers needed an answer.

"Mary?"

Mary sat upright and brought her thoughts into focus. "I'll try. I-I will do what I can," she stammered.

"That's the spirit. I'll let the Baughers know you've agreed."

The day of the funeral arrived. Papa drove Mama and Mary four miles to the little white Brethren Church at the edge of the small town of Bridgewater. Mary twiddled her thumbs as Papa leaped out of the buggy and tied Pet under a large tree. Then Papa swept her to the ground, and turned back so he could assist Mama from the buggy.

Buggies followed single file through the fallen leaves in the driveway. While the men tied horses to hitching posts the women gathered at the church doors and visited in low, sober tones. The funeral director guided Mary to the cluster of girl pallbearers. Together they waited until the casket had been brought.

Mary took hold of the handle and together the foursome slowly edged toward the church with the casket between them. Mary saw the four steps. Could she make it? This casket was much heavier than she had imagined.

She took one step up. The weight of the casket was astounding. She took another step. Could she do it? Her upper leg pressed deeply into the wooden limb. A third step up. She sighed and placed her foot on the top step. Could she do the last step? Her legs trembled under the weight of the casket. She held tightly to the casket and with all her might pulled the wooden limb up. She did it! She had gone four steps on a wooden leg.

Somehow she made her way with the others to the front of the church and sat down. Why had God allowed this? She really could not understand. The preacher said we cannot always understand God's ways, but we must still trust Him, even in the difficulties.

Yes, she agreed. She did not know why God had spared her own life and taken Alta's. Nor did she understand why God had allowed her to lose a limb. But God was good and cared about her life . . . and Alta's. She must trust God. He knows best.

When the sermon ended, the four young girls carried the casket down the aisle and steps. Mary walked carefully, trying hard to keep her balance and make her wooden limb swing forward in time with the other girls' walking. Step, swing the limb. Step, swing the limb. Hang onto the casket, she told herself. You're almost there.

The last step was made and the casket put down. She stepped back, sighed, and rubbed her aching hands and trembling legs. She had done it! No one had really known how difficult it had been. But she had done it!

She looked over at Papa and Mama. They were looking at her, not smiling, but with approval. She knew they were pleased with her.

People dabbed at their eyes, whispered comforting words to the Baugher family, and parted. Mary took one more look at the casket and walked toward the buggy with Papa and Mama. She felt Papa's big hand slip over her own. When she looked up at him, he was wiping his eyes with a white handkerchief. Suddenly she realized now was her chance to ask about walking to school.

"Papa, may I walk to school tomorrow?"

"Think you can?"

"Yes, Papa. Did you see what I did today?"

"I saw," Papa said swinging her up into the buggy. He turned and helped Mama up into the buggy.

"I suppose you may, Mary," Papa answered while untying the horse.

She beamed up at Mama, but Mama was dabbing her pretty handkerchief at her eyes. Papa leaped into the buggy and clicked at Pet to get going.

Mary leaned forward and peered toward the graveyard where a few people still lingered. She saw the new-made mound topped with a cluster of flowers. Alta was in heaven, she knew, and never would know pain or sorrow, or even of difficulty walking ever again.

We cannot always understand God's ways,
but we must still trust Him,
even in the difficulties.

19

One-Half-Mile on Wood

Mary swung her lunch pail by her side as she walked between Ella and John. Up ahead she saw the cluster of Shifflet children bobbing up and down awaiting the arrival of herself, John and Ella.

She plodded forward trying to go faster. There was Stella waving her hand high. She raised her hand in response to Stella. Mary limped slightly as she walked. Would Stella be ashamed to arrive at school with her?

Soon she and her brother and sister joined the Shifflets, chatting eagerly as they skipped along the wooded river trail leading to the swinging bridge. A squirrel scampered in front of her and Stella.

"Look at him go," giggled Stella.

"Could we catch him?" Mary asked, quickening her pace.

The squirrel stopped, then scurried away. But she had chased him. And now she was walking to school with Stella! Maybe she could be normal after all.

On they trudged through the trees where red and

golden trees dropped leaves over the pathway.
Together they climbed the plank to the swinging
bridge. Mary stepped forward watching John and the
other Shifflet children near the middle of the bridge.
Like a great balloon, happiness swelled within her
heart. Could it really be true that she was walking to
school with her wooden leg? She followed them to the
center of the long bridge.

Suddenly she felt the swinging bridge lurch
violently up and down. She grabbed tightly to the
cable, steadying herself.

"You boys stop that!" Stella shouted from behind
Mary.

Mary looked from one end of the bridge to the
other. On the other end, boys were jumping up and
down, making a rippling effect to the bridge. She
clung desperately to the rope, so as not to lose her
balance.

"Stop it!" Ella said firmly. "Mary doesn't have
two legs like us to balance on."

"Aw-w, all right," the boys muttered, their heads
dropping in disappointment.

But Mary had balanced herself and caught onto
the game the boys were playing. She gave a little
bounce and the bridge wavered. She bounced again
making a stronger sway to the bridge. The boys and
girls watched Mary with mouths open in amaze-
ment.

"Look at her!"

"She's no different than us."

"I don't want to be babied," Mary said firmly,
giving a stronger bounce that joggled the bridge
almost as much as the boys had.

The children nodded in agreement and took off for the schoolhouse. She and Stella followed not far behind. The limb ached somewhat, but she was almost there. She could do it! Soon the discomfort would cease when she sat in her desk.

The distance shortened and soon she was climbing the school steps. She had done it! And Stella didn't seem ashamed of her. Even the other children had accepted her.

She was almost there. She could do it!

Mary made her way into the schoolhouse and sat down in her seat. Whew! What relief to sit and rest. But she had done it!

The teacher walked to the door and rang the bell. Soon boys and girls bustled through the door, panting from play, and dropped into their seats. The class was called to order and the academic day begun.

Mary dug into her books earnestly. And when the water bucket was brought around, she sipped a drink from the dipper just like everyone else.

Reading, writing, arithmetic, and play sped the day away. She had played games just like others and almost as good as they. She joined the chatter of children fresh out of school and headed homeward. On the road ahead, Bill Flemings approached them. He did not seem so frightening anymore. She waved at him and he waved back. Why he is even friendly, she thought.

She and Stella walked across the swinging bridge and down the plank. A few late blossoms which had escaped frost persisted in blooming along the trail. Mary and Stella eagerly gathered them to take home. Mama would love a bouquet for the table. Mary picked up her lunch pail and bouquet and took off behind Stella. Hoppity hop. Hoppity hop.

"You better not do that," Stella giggled turning around to watch Mary. "Those blossoms will all fall off till you get home."

Mary caught up with Stella. Together they made their way through the river trail and out into the sunny meadow. Soon they arrived at Stella's home and waved good-bye to each other.

"See you tomorrow," Mary called as she walked

homeward.

John, Ella, and Annie were already home. She peered toward the barn where Papa and her brothers were likely at work. Her gaze shifted back to the square, neat house. Maybe Mama had baked bread today. Maybe Papa would churn butter tonight and sing holding Mabel on his knee.

She trudged on. Her leg was aching, but she was almost home. She could do it. She would do it! Again her eyes scanned the farm. Grandmother was no longer a part of their home. My, how she missed Grandmother! There was the springhouse where Grandfather made the pipelines from tree branches. Maybe Maggie was weaving today. She would have to visit the loom room and see.

Mary looked down to see if the blossoms were still intact. Most of them were. She turned into the yard. She had done it . . . she and her helpful wooden leg. What would God have in store for her and her wooden leg in the future? She did not know.

She pushed onward across the yard in spite of her throbbing limb. She looked up at the kitchen window where Papa and Mama stood watching her with smiles on their faces. She could hardly wait to tell them of her walk to school. She hurried up the steps. Home. Wonderful home! Papa was holding the door open for her.

"Papa! Papa, I did it!" she exclaimed.

"Yes, you did," Papa said, clasping her to himself. A broad grin crept over his face.

Mama slipped around from behind Papa and took the bouquet from Mary.

"Thank you for the lovely bouquet. It will look

nice on our supper table," Mama said smiling.

Mary looked from Papa to Mama. Such love as she had never known swelled within her. But she could never explain it to them. She looked over her shoulder and noticed the kitchen door still stood open. She stretched her wooden leg forward, hooked the toes under the bottom edge of the door and pulled it shut behind herself. One-half-mile on wood. What couldn't she and that wooden leg do?

END

Appendix

Records From Maggie Rohrer Koogler

Editing has been kept to a minimum so as to retain the record Maggie kept. Changes consist of spelling out abbreviations or use of a comma rather than a dash for consistency throughout the record. Numerical calendar days were recorded in the original record along with an occasional day of the week. Most of the days of the week (Monday, Tuesday, etc.) were added by the author for clarity of the record.

August 12, 1908 — On Wednesday evening, our little sister, Mary Rohrer, aged five years—was out with our brothers grinding feed with a horse drawn grinder, she was riding on the tongue—in glee—Then it happened—soon her foot caught. Pulled it off just above the ankle.

Three Doctors came—Turner, Ralston, and Payne. They worked faithful for hours. Took it off three inches below the knee. They worked by lamp light in our home.

People to see Mary when she was hurt.

Wednesday evening, August 12, 1908 — Three Doctors — Turner, Ralston and Payne operated in the home by lamp light. Henry, Uncle Will and Aunt Bettie Rhodes, Otis and Ada Shifflet, Bud Whitmore, John Shank, Aldine Knicely — came.

Thursday, August 13, 1908 — Doctor Turner, John Shank, Aldine Knicely, Aunt Rebecca and Paul Shank, Uncle Dan Showalters, Annie Burkholder, Lelia Rhodes, Isaac Kulp, Myrtle Shifflet, Fannie Suthard, Bessie Ashenfelter, Joe Kulp, Perry Wenger, Mrs. Henry Shickel and Johnny, Joe Heatwole, George Shifflett, Harry and Mabel Showalter, and two western girls.

Friday, August 14 — Doctor Turner, Preacher Simeon Heatwole, Henry and Bertie, Mary and Susie Kulp, Florence and Myrtie Knicely, Uncle Sam Burkholders.

Saturday, August 15 — Doctor Turner, Joe Coffman, Isaac Kulps, Effie and Sallie Wheelbarger, Annie and Grace Cowger, Lizzie and Sallie Heatwole, Aunt Rebecca and Will Shanks.

Sunday, August 16 — Doctor Turner, Uncle Will Rhodeses, Mrs. Connie Miller, Mrs. Swartz, Annie Burkholder, Henry and Bertie, Uncle Sam Burkholders and Belle Fulk, Jake Coffmans, John Showalter, Mattie, Hilbert, Raleigh, and Jesse Rhodes, Uncle Perry Shank, Preacher Abraham (Abe) Burkholders, Ida Rhodes, Edna Heatwole, Stella Shifflett.

Monday, August 17 — Doctor Turner, Sallie Keller, Hannah Shank, Lucy and Mollie Flemings, Stella Shifflett.

Tuesday, August 18 — Doctor Turner, Aldine Knicely, Henry.

Wednesday, August 19 — Frank Denton, Sallie Knicely and baby, Mary Showalter, Bertha and Eula Knicely.

Thursday, August 20 — Doctor Turner, Otis, Wade, and Stella Shifflett, Emory, Ruth and Hazel Heatwole, Sallie and Della Weaver, Lucy and Mollie Flemings, Frank and Ruth Denton, Christ Kulp, Uncle Dan Showalters, Henry and Bertie.

Friday, August 21 — Isaac Kulp, Grace and Ethel Heatwole, Cousin Fannie Rhodes, Nina Riddel, Abe Simmers.

Saturday, August 22 — Doctor Turner, Preacher Gabriel (Gabe) Heatwole, Ada (Shifflett) Wenger and children, Florence Knicely and children.

Sunday, August 23 — Ervin Kooglers and Naomi, Henry and Bertie, Nellie Suthard, Eliza Clayton, Christ, Mary, and Susie Kulp, John Moseman, Frainie Coffman, Joe Coffman's and Nellie, Mabel Showalter.

Monday, August 24 — Myrtie, Tracy, and Louetta Knicely.

Wednesday, August 26 — Doctor Turner, Nellie Coffman, Bertie, Aunt Rebecca Shank, Iva Rhodes, Myrtle Shifflett and children.

Thursday, August 27 — Henry, Ida, and Vera Early, Dannie and Michael Showalter.

Friday, August 28 — Beckie and Mary Hartman, Lucy and Mollie Flemings.

Saturday, August 29 — Henry and Bertie, Will Flemings, Fannie and Mary Shank, Nellie Suthard, Bessie Ashenfelter, Myrtie Knicely, Preacher Gabriel (Gabe) Heatwole.

Sunday, August 30 — Emory Heatwole, Lewis Goods, Amos Shank, Uncle Dan Showalters and boys, Edna, Calvin, Annie and Effie Heatwole.

Monday, August 31 — Fannie Wenger and mother, Frank Denton, John Ashenfelter.

Tuesday, September — Oliver Burkholders, Christ Kulp and mother, Bud Whitmore, Lucy and Mollie Flemings.

Wednesday, September 2 — Doctor Turner was here the last time.

Thursday, September 3 — Lydia Arey, Harry and Mary Showalter.

Friday, September 4 — Lucy and Mollie Flemings.

Saturday, September 6 — Henry and Bertie.

Sunday, September 7 — Mamie, Hattie, and Libby Whitmore.

Doctor's Charges

Doctor Turner — 11 trips, $28.50 in all — operation, $15.00.
Doctor Ralston — $10.00
Doctor Payne — $5.00
Total expense — $53.50

Sept 22nd 1908

Mr Isreal Rohrer

To Ashby Turner, M.D. Dr.
Hinton, Va.

TERMS

1908	accident Aug. 12		
Aug 12	To one visit & operation	$15.00	
" 13	" " "	1.50	
" 14	" " "	1.50	
" 15	" " "	1.50	
" 16	" " "	1.50	
" 18	" " "	1.50	
" 20	" " "	1.50	
" 22	" " "	1.50	
" 26	" " "	1.50	
Sept 2	" " "	1.50	
	Total	$28.50	

Actual document of Doctor Turner's charges.

(Courtesy of Maggie Koogler)

To My Crippled Sister

'Twas on a summer evening,
   The sun was sinking low,
We children were gathered round the farm,
   The evening chores to do.

No one thought of danger,
   As we hurried to and fro.
The day passed on and night drew near;
   As they usually come and go.

Our brothers were grinding feed,
   Close by the granary gate.
And there our little sister
   Met with her sad fate.

She had ventured into danger;
   And no one understood.
They thought it was safe for her to ride
   On the beams where the horses trod.

She laughed and sang as she rode around,
   And I heard her voice so dear,
As I passed along to the meadow grass
   To feed a lamb that was near.

My first thoughts were to take her along,
   And I never will forget
The sight I saw when I came back,
   Oft' times I can see it yet.

Poor little Mary had lost her foot
   In the grinder's cruel vise,
As she held tight with her little hands,
   Thinking to save her life.

We heard her screams and all came near,
   And this is what we found.
Mother and sister carrying her in,
   As the blood dropped to the ground.

God sent an angel to minister to her;
  For she said she had no pain,
And wanted to go to her little bed,
  And sleep until morning came.

In haste the doctor was summoned;
  Then he said he needed two more.
They did what they could by the lamplight there,
  Her mangled limb to restore.

For many days she suffered;
  And we watched with tender care,
As her faithful doctor came each day,
  And dressed it with skill that was rare.

Dear Mother's grief was hard to bear;
  Her tender heart ached with pain,
As over and over again she said,
  "Poor little Mary will never walk again."

But her father said he had a plan;
  And this is how he cared,
"As soon as she is strong enough,
  No money will be spared."

He took her to the city,
  Where he stayed with a friend.
From there they went to the factory,
  This was their journey's end.

Here they fitted limbs for little girls,
  The same as for women and men.
*And our father told of the **happy smile***
  *When **Mary** could walk again.*

Composed by your sister,
January 5, 1948
Anna May Rhodes

The Author

Janis Good, her husband, and four children live on a dairy farm in the heart of the Shenandoah Valley of Virginia. She is an active homemaker, farm wife, mother and writer. In 1977 she married her husband, John. Her writing generally depicts the quieter lifestyle of rural living. She is also an avid lover of history which is reflected in her recent writings.

Janis and her family are actively involved in a small mission church tucked under the foot of a blue mountain ridge.